She speaks with wisdom,

and faithful instruction is on her tongue.

She watches over the affairs of her household ...

—Proverbs 31:26–27

ZONDERKIDZ

The Berenstain Bears' Perfect Fishing Spot

Copyright © 1992, 2011 by Berenstain Publishing, Inc.
Illustrations © 1992, 2011 by Berenstain Publishing, Inc.

Requests for information should be addressed to:
Zonderkidz, *Grand Rapids, Michigan 49530*

Library of Congress Cataloging-in-Publication Data

Berenstain, Stan, 1923–2005
  The Berenstain Bears' perfect fishing spot / created by Stan & Jan Berenstain
with Mike Berenstain.
      p.   cm.
  Summary: Dad and the cubs try to catch a fish for dinner with humorous results.
  ISBN 978-0-310-72276-2 (softcover)
  [1. Stories in rhyme. 2. Fishing—Fiction. 3. Bears—Fiction.] I. Berenstain, Jan,
1923- II. Berenstain, Mike, 1951- III. Title.
  PZ8.3.B4493Bhij   2011
  [E]—dc22   2010028357

Editor: *Mary Hassinger*
Art direction: *Cindy Davis*

Printed in China

11 12 13 14 15 16 /SCC/ 10 9 8 7 6 5 4 3 2 1

The Berenstain Bears'
PERFECT
FISHING
SPOT

by Stan and Jan Berenstain
with Mike Berenstain

ZONDERVAN.com/
AUTHORTRACKER
follow your favorite authors

ZONDERkidz

Living
Lights™

Beginning Reader

Do you know what I wish?
I wish that for dinner
we could have fish.

A fine, fat fish, tender and sweet.
There is nothing better
in the world to eat!
Thanks be to God
for that delicious treat!

A fish would be fine.
But there's no need to fuss.
Just go and buy one
from Grizzly Gus.

May Sister and I come with you, Dad?

Yes, indeed.
Of course, my lad.
Spending time with you two
makes my heart glad!

But, Papa!
Ma said go to Grizzly Gus!

That's true, my son.
But just between us,
if you want a fish
that's tender and sweet,
a fish that's a wonderful treat
for a bear to eat—

then dig up some worms,
get out your pole,

GRIZZLY
FISH

and head for your favorite
fishing hole.

Your fishing hole
looks small, Papa Bear.
Can there really be
a big fish in there?

Of course there can.
I've got one now!
Just watch your dad.
He'll show you how
to catch a fish
that's tender and sweet,
a fish that's a treat
for a bear to eat!

Papa, that fish
may be tender and sweet,
but it's much too small
for us to eat.

Hmm. The big ones have all
been caught, you see,
caught years ago
by guess who? ME!

I know a better
fishing spot!

I can taste that fish,
tender, hot,
a fish to do
our family proud...

But Pa, it says
NO FISHING ALLOWED!

But who will know
if I drop my hook?

He will, Pa!
The fish warden! Look!

I see, I see.
Good day to you!
Er...my cubs and I
were enjoying the view!
So sorry! God bless!
Such a good job you do!

This fish, Dad,
will you catch it soon?
I think it must be
after noon!

Don't bother me
with questions, please.
I know a spot
just past those trees!

Look, cubs! Look!
I've got a bite!
Whatever I've hooked,
just look at it fight!

Look how it thrashes!
Look how it sloshes!

Dad, that isn't a fish!
It's a pair of galoshes!

This way, cubs!
Follow me!
We will get our fish
from the deep blue sea!
God provides, he'll make sure
we have what we need!

BOATS RENTED

Look at them all!
They'll sink our boat!
Throw 'em back!
We must stay afloat!

Help! Help!
Look, Papa Bear!
We're going up!
Up in the air!

Boat and all!
In a great big net!
We're in the air
and very wet!

We're coming down
on a great big boat—
the biggest
fishing boat afloat!

You got caught with our fish.
Sorry about that!
Excuse me, sir—
but that's one of ours
under your hat!

Pa, we still have
a fish to get!
We have not caught
our dinner yet!

No problem, son.
No need to fuss!
We'll buy our fish
from Grizzly Gus!

My best advice
to both of you
is to do what Mama
says to do!

God's blessed Gus with
the perfect fishing spot.
We never really
had a shot.

Ah! A fish that's tender.
A fish that's sweet.
A fish that's good
for a bear family to eat!
God bless this food.
God bless this treat!